Leah the Lion

Chip Spangler
Ephesians 4:32

Written by Cheryl Sperry Golke

golke.cheryl@gmail.com

Illustrated by Nifty Illustration

www.niftyillustration.com

niftyillustration@mail.com

ISBN: 978-1-54391-426-9

To my Angels

Dear Little Ones,

Is there something you are good at? Those things are called "gifts" or "talents." Everyone has them. Our gifts and talents are given to us by God. Each of us must learn to use our gifts and talents in the right way, helping others. We must be careful we never use them to show off or hurt someone else's feelings. Leah the Lion had to learn that lesson the hard way. By only thinking about herself, she annoyed everyone around her. Thankfully, her little sister was able to open her eyes, and Leah made up with all her friends again. Her friends forgave Leah, just like God forgives us and we must forgive others.

I hope you enjoy reading Leah the Lion!

Leah the Lion loved to practice her roar.

She'd roar and she'd roar, and then she'd roar some more!

When she looked down, she roared at the grass.

She roared at the bugs, she roared at the ants.

She roared at the flowers, she roared at the bees.

She roared at the birds,

she roared at the trees.

She roared at the sun, but that hurt her eyes!

She roared at the moon, but her mother said,

"Leah, please come inside!"

She roared through the day and she roared late at night.

Her mother said, "Leah, please turn out that light!"

She roared at the table. She roared at her food.

Her sister asked, "Leah, why are you always in such a bad mood?"

At school, Leah roared on the playground at the kids playing there.

Slide, swing and sandbox, she roared everywhere!

She roared at the girls and she roared at the guys.

She roared at the 4th graders two times her size!

"That Leah's a grouch!" the other kids said.

They all wondered, "Why? Did she hit her head?"

"She's no fun to play with," the kids told their teacher.

Their teacher said, "Children, there must be some way to reach her!"

Leah didn't know that it was because of her roar

when the kids all picked teams she was always ignored.

She cried, "Why don't I have any friends anymore?"

Then one day a Lion girl down the street was having a birthday, and her mother thought that it would be neat to invite the whole school, the girls and the boys.

But the lion girl said, "Not that girl who makes noise!"

The day was approaching, all the kids were excited!

Leah checked the mail every day, but she was not invited.

Leah was so sad she flopped down on her bed, then she
pulled the pillow up over her head. She squeaked out a roar
into the fluff.

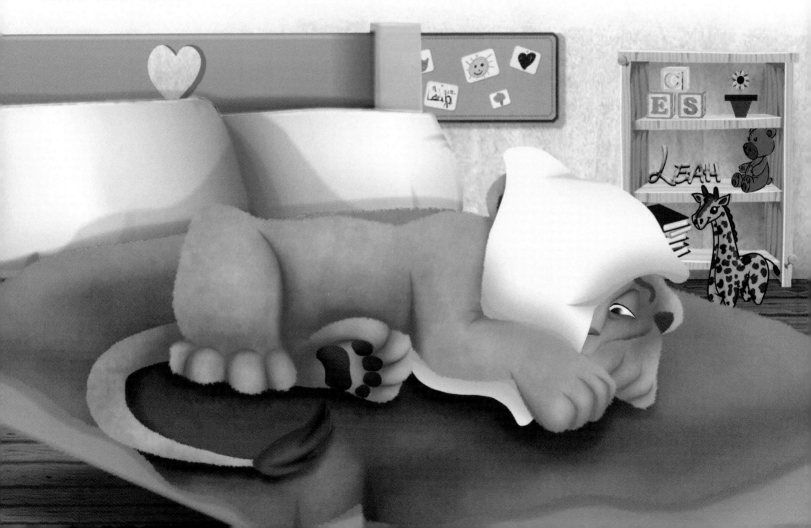

Her sister walked by carrying presents and stuff.

"Leah, I wish that you could come too!

"I have an idea for what you could do..."

Leah asked, "Why don't the kids like me anymore?"

Her sister stopped then and stood by the door.

"It's because of the roaring, and nothing more! The kids do not

like to be roared at when they swing and they slide! When they

see you coming, they all want to hide!

Then Leah's eyes filled with tears, she was so sad.

She didn't know that so much roaring was bad!

Her sister said, "Please don't cry, Leah, you had not a clue!

But I have an idea for what you could do!"

Leah's bottom lip trembled and she gave a big sniff.

Then she decided to listen to her little sis.

Her sister said, "Leah, no one, but no one roars as good as you!

Why don't you show them just what you do?"

"Would the kids really like that?" Leah thought to herself.

"If they did, maybe I would not always have to roar by myself!"

So the next day at school the kids gathered around, and Leah showed them all how she made that loud sound.

But first she told them, "I'm sorry!"

And she really meant it too!

"I just love roaring so much! I can't do just a few!"

"That's ok, Leah!" the kids answered then.

"We all still like you! Let's all be friends!"

So Leah showed the way that she roared to all the girls and the guys. She even showed the 4th graders two times her size!

Then the kids all decided that they'd like to try, and their teacher came out and said,

"Well, my, my, my..."

The kids all looked down and roared at the grass.

They roared at the bugs,

they roared at the ants.

They roared at the flowers,

they roared at the bees.

They roared at the birds,

they roared at the trees.

Leah said, "Wait, don't roar at the sun!"

And the kids were all laughing and having such fun!

They were roaring and roaring and roaring a ton!

Then Leah looked around, and what do you know?

She had more friends than she could count on all her

fingers and toes!

TEAM GAIL